For Matthew, Aiden, Audrey Anna, and Amelia Claire.
May your butterflies always dance.

Revised edition

First paperback edition January 2021

ISBN (paperback): 978-1-954041-01-1
ISBN (hardback): 978-1-954041-00-4
ISBN (ebook): 978-1-954041-02-8

Published by Creative Sound Press
www.creativesoundpress.com
publishing@creativesoundpress.com

Hannabelle's Butterflies

Charlene A. Ryan

Hannabelle had the loveliest singing voice in all of Valley Woods. Everyone said so. When she opened her heart to sing, all those around her simply had to stop and listen.

Hannabelle LOVED to sing. She sang in the shower. She sang in the car. She sang while she daydreamed, did homework, and made her bed.

It was rare to see Hannabelle without a tune on her lips.

In all of Hannabelle's world, there was only one place
where she did NOT love to sing.

And that was
ON STAGE
IN FRONT OF PEOPLE.

Which was, at this moment, a problem.
The school variety show was coming up and everyone
expected Hannabelle to sing.

Hannabelle was scared to sing in front of all those people, all by herself. She didn't like the way her hands got all clammy and cold. She didn't like the way her heart beat so fast she could feel it pounding in her chest.

And she didn't like the way her mind played tricks on her, telling her she
WASN'T READY,
WASN'T GOOD ENOUGH,
and
NO ONE WOULD WANT TO LISTEN.

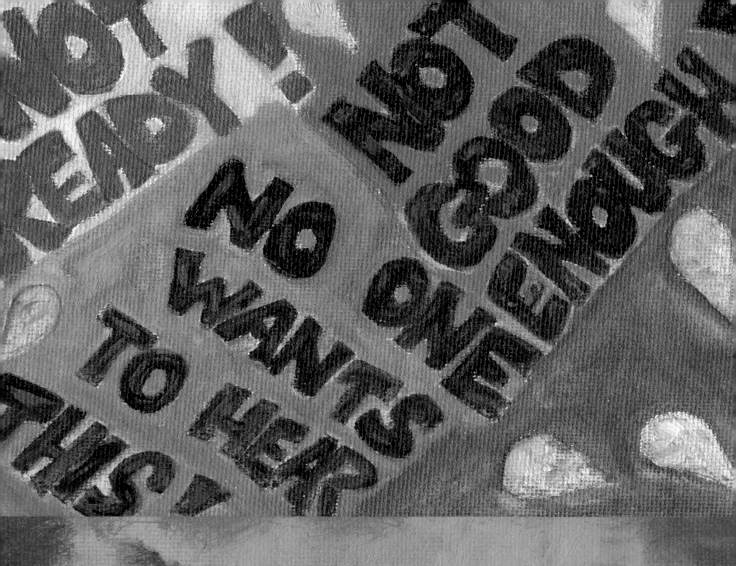

Hannabelle knew that she WAS prepared and sounded terrific... But when it was time to put herself out there, she was never quite sure.

Hannabelle LOVED to SING.
She just
DIDN'T
LOVE
TO
PERFORM.

fortunately for her, Hannabelle's friends had a plan. They all LOVED MUSIC. And they really, really loved getting together to make music, every Saturday morning at Hannabelle's house.

The variety show had been all they could talk about for weeks, and they decided to make this Saturday, the last one before the show, a DRESS REHEARSAL.

Hannabelle, Roxy, Waverly,
Stokely, Bastien, and Octavia
(to outsiders, the unlikeliest
of friends) set up milk crates
in front of the piano, with a
little aisle in the middle.

One by one they pulled names
out of a hat to decide the
order of performers. Then
everyone took their seats and
got ready to begin...

Roxy's name was drawn first, and they couldn't have planned a better person to get things rolling.

It had taken a long time and a lot of careful listening to figure the whole song out from the recording, but her friends agreed it was definitely worth it.

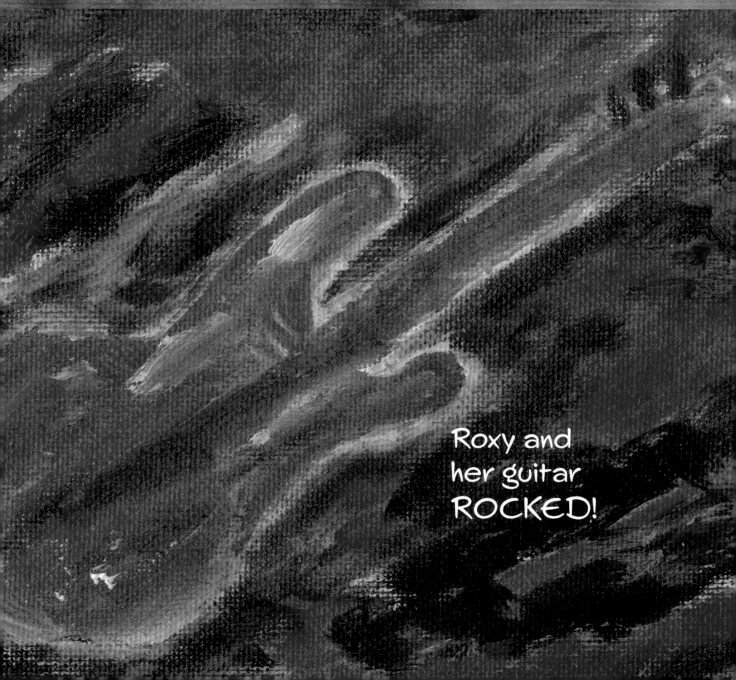

Roxy and her guitar ROCKED!

AND

WOKE

HANNABELLE'S

BUTTERFLIES!

Waverly was next.

By the time his turn came he was EXPLODING
with energy. His drumsticks moved from snare
to tom, crash to high hat, while his foot kept
the bass drum thumping.

The rhythms were infectious!

Around the room six heads bobbed
and twelve feet tapped.

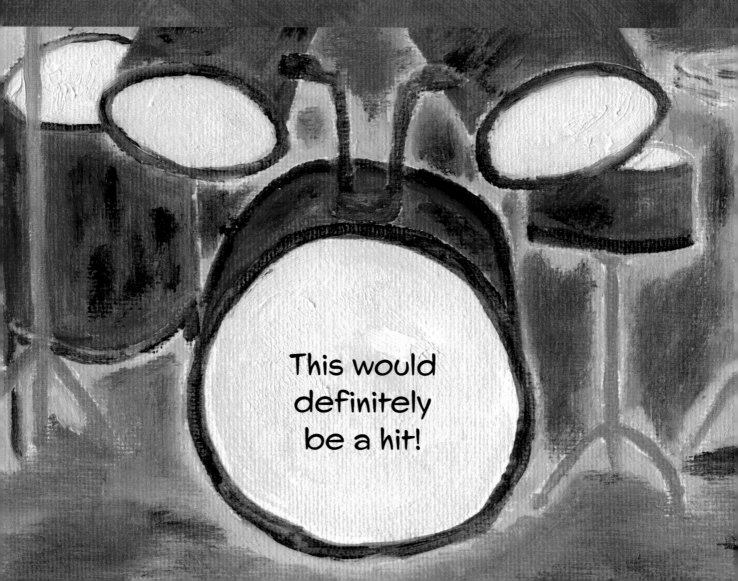

This would
definitely
be a hit!

Stokely sang a lovely old ballad.

He'd known it since he was
little and it was one of his
favorites. Until now, he had
only sung it for his baby sister.

Everyone agreed— there wouldn't
be a dry eye in the hall.

Bastien played a rollicking piece he'd learned from his grandad—but he had a surprise for his friends...

Right in the middle, he let go of his accordion, pulled a harmonica out of his pocket, and played a riff of his very own!

Bastien was SO creative!

Octavia played a jazzy tune her teacher had picked especially for the show. With her eyes closed, she pretended that she was in a grand concert hall.

She even wore her concert dress.

Octavia was very excited!

And so it seemed that everyone was awaiting
the arrival of the big night.

Everyone, that is,
except Hannabelle.

Hannabelle wasn't excited about it at all.

In fact,
she wasn't even
sure she wanted
to do it.

But she took a deep breath
and sang her song anyway...

And her friends said it was so beautiful—how could she NOT share it with the whole school?

They were so certain and so sure that Hannabelle just smiled and thanked them. She was lucky to have such good friends.

But that didn't stop her from feeling anxious.

On the night of the show, Mr. Starling gathered the students in the hall an hour before showtime. Hannabelle's butterflies were fluttering around in her stomach. She tried not to think about them, but the harder she tried, the more active they became.

The audience would soon be here.

HANNABELLE
WONDERED
IF SHE HAD
MADE A
BIG MISTAKE.

All around
her, kids were
gearing up for
their turn in the
spotlight.

Hannabelle noticed Stokely
sitting alone in the back row
of the auditorium.

She went to sit with him.

Maybe being with a
friend would help
calm her nerves.

"Hi Stokely," she said. "What are you doing back here all by yourself?"

"Pretending I'm at home, singing my little sister to sleep.

It helps me to focus on my song, instead of on all the people."

Hannabelle didn't want to interrupt Stokely's imagining, so she soon left.

She heard familiar guitar sounds coming from a classroom and peeked inside. Roxy was there, tuning her guitar with a giant grin on her face. She even let out a little giggle!

How could she be feeling so happy right before showtime?

"I'm picturing the audience all sitting there in their underwear!" said Roxy, when Hannabelle asked.

"It helps me to relax. You'd laugh, too, if you could see Mr. McIntyre's purple polka dots!"

(It might help you to know that Mr. McIntyre was the kids' least favorite teacher. It seemed like waking up on the right side of the bed was a daily challenge for him...)

With the image of purple
underpants blazing in her
mind, Hannabelle left Roxy
to continue prepping.

She went to the waterfountain for
a drink, and there she bumped into
Waverly. In his hand was a picture of his
parents and his big sister. Hannabelle
thought this was a pretty unusual thing
to be carrying around.

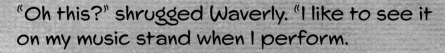

"Oh this?" shrugged Waverly. "I like to see it on my music stand when I perform.

It helps me remember to play like I do when it's just my family listening, even if there are lots of other people there."

Hannabelle took a long, thoughtful drink and headed back inside.

She soon spied Octavia leaning back in her chair with her eyes closed. Hannabelle figured she would sit with her and try to calm down.

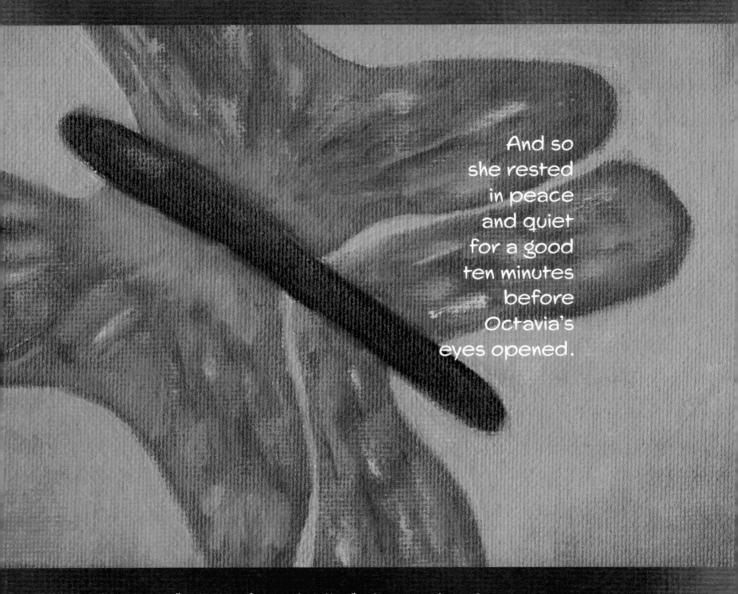

And so she rested in peace and quiet for a good ten minutes before Octavia's eyes opened.

"Oh, hi Hannabelle!" she said with surprise. "I didn't know you were here. I was doing a little last minute practice."

Huh? thought Hannabelle. Maybe she'd heard her wrong. There was no piano in sight.

"Oh, I always do a practice performance in my mind before I go onstage," explained Octavia. "I start backstage: my name is called. I walk onstage and see everyone smiling up at me. I feel great, the piano feels perfect, and I play my absolute best.

It really helps me get ready."

The lights in the hall blinked three times—five minutes to showtime! Leaving Octavia to her practice, Hannabelle headed to the restroom for a final visit. On the way, she passed Bastien, laughing and joking in a circle of friends.

What on Earth...? thought Hannabelle.

"Bastien!" she demanded, "How can you be standing there laughing and joking just minutes before the show?!"

"Well..." replied Bastien, somewhat matter-of-factly.

"What else is there to do?
There's no point in standing around
worrying about my performance. That
won't do me or the music any good. I
might as well have some fun now so that
I can walk onstage feeling great.

I always do it this way."

Hannabelle was stunned.

She thought she was the only
one with butterflies in her
stomach. The only one who felt
that performing onstage was
different from singing for her
family or friends.

But it turns out that
everyone knows. And they
all have a plan. A plan for
making beautiful music,
in spite of those pesky
butterflies!

Hannabelle
needed a
moment
to process
this revelation.

She walked
slowly back to
the hall, deep in
thought.

Hannabelle thought about her parents who would be smiling up at her from the front row.

And about her friends who believed in her so well.

She thought about all the times she had sung her song so beautifully and how good it had made her feel.

She thought about
Mr. McIntyre...

and his purple polka-dotted
underpants.

She thought
about
walking
onstage
confidently
and
proudly.

And singing her very
best.

THEN...
she stood up
straight
and
TALL
and smiled
her biggest
smile.

Mr. Starling had just
called her name.

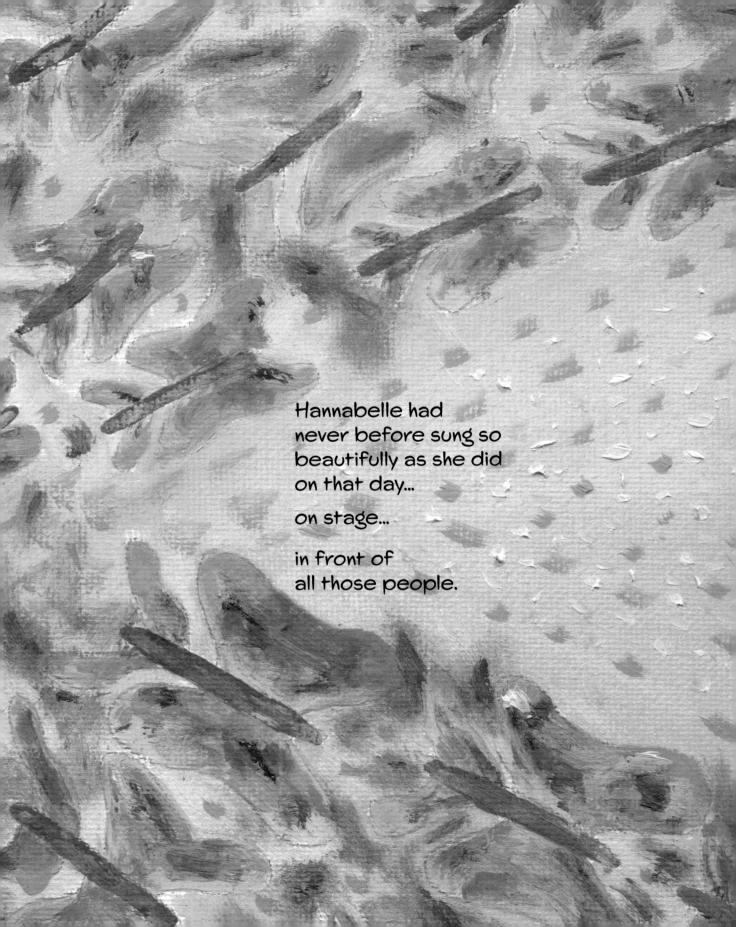

Hannabelle had
never before sung so
beautifully as she did
on that day...

on stage...

in front of
all those people.

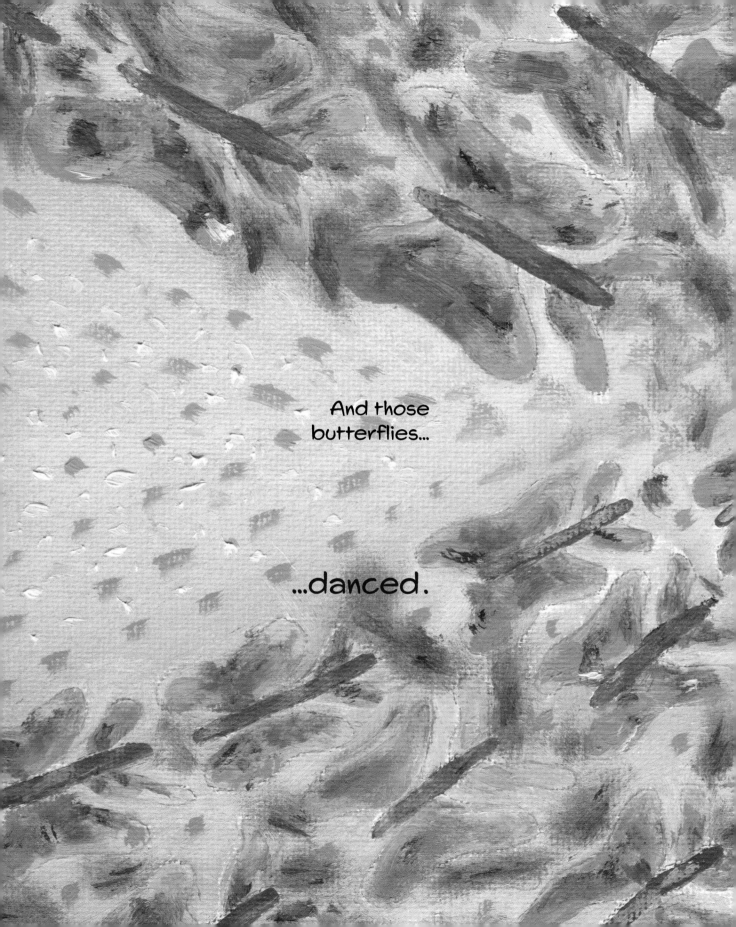

And those
butterflies...

...danced.

Charlene A. Ryan is a musician,
painter, writer, and mom. She
has spent most of her life behind
an instrument and in front of an
audience of one kind or another.

To learn more about Hannabelle's
(and other kids') butterflies visit
www.charlenearyan.com